Be sure to be a good friend,

Enjoy!

windhillbooks*
windhillbooks.com

Published in August, 2016 by Windhill Books LLC, Onalaska, WI 54650. windhillbooks.com
ISBN 978-1-944734-00-8 | Library of Congress Control Number: 2016912876 | Printed in the USA

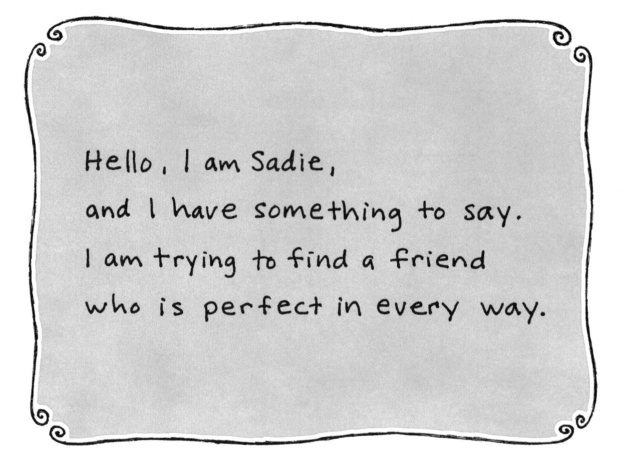

Hello, I am Sadie,
and I have something to say.
I am trying to find a friend
who is perfect in every way.

These are the things
I had in mind,
but a perfect friend
is hard to find...

When I met Olive
it was friends at first sight.

Soon I saw

something was not right.

Olive had games, toys,
and dolls with curly hair.
Her problem was:
she would not share.

Playing with her
was not much fun.
I got half a doll...

and she got 101!

Saturday afternoon
I played in the park.

Along came a boy
who liked to bark!

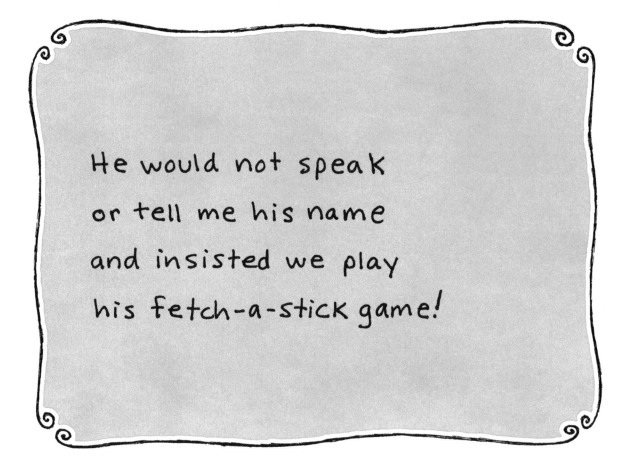

He would not speak
or tell me his name
and insisted we play
his fetch-a-stick game!

Our friendship did not last.
It quickly turned sour
when he spotted a hound
and chased her for an hour!

Melody and I
enjoyed singing songs.

But she always left me
when a new friend came along.

I met a cheerful boy
swimming in the lake.
But his strong smell
left fish in his wake!

At first, I thought
he seemed really nice.
Then I noticed
he smelled like onion and spice.
I was sure he ate them raw.
I could not bear to look.

He tried to explain—
his dad was a gourmet cook.

The curly-haired girl
I met at the mall
tended to act
like she knew it all.

whenever I showed her
I learned something new.

she quickly reminded me
that she had too!

My new friend Harry
had a popular magic show.
He asked me into his
vanishing box,
but I quickly said, "No!"

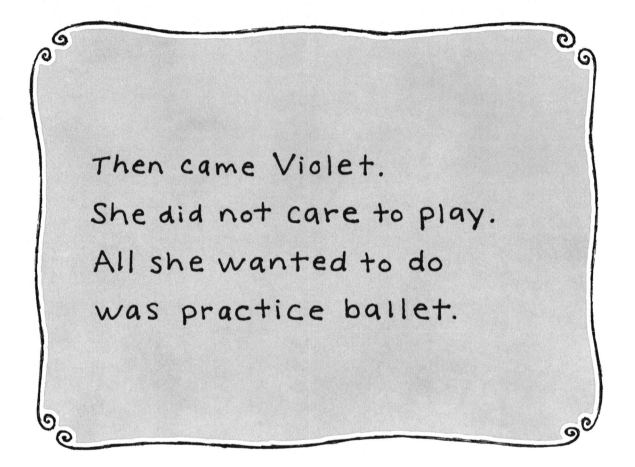

Then came Violet.
She did not care to play.
All she wanted to do
was practice ballet.

I met a sweet boy
on the park bench,
but we could not chat
because he only spoke French!

Beth was nice
and really quite charming,
but she was only interested
in organic farming.

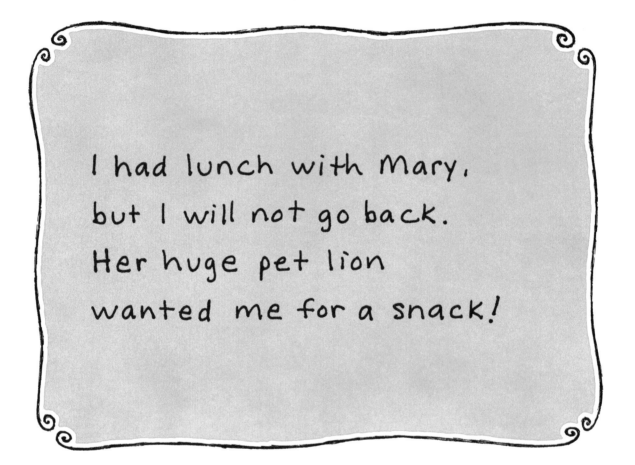

I had lunch with Mary,
but I will not go back.
Her huge pet lion
wanted me for a snack!

Next I met Chloe.
We got along well.
Soon I found myself
under her spell.

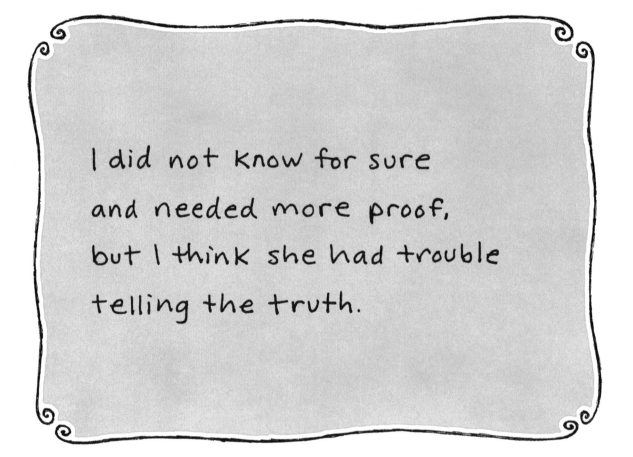

I did not know for sure
and needed more proof,
but I think she had trouble
telling the truth.

Chloe told me her friends were famous movie stars who drove her around town in their big, fancy cars!

So... The secret to friendship
seems to be:
to find a good friend,
it starts with me.

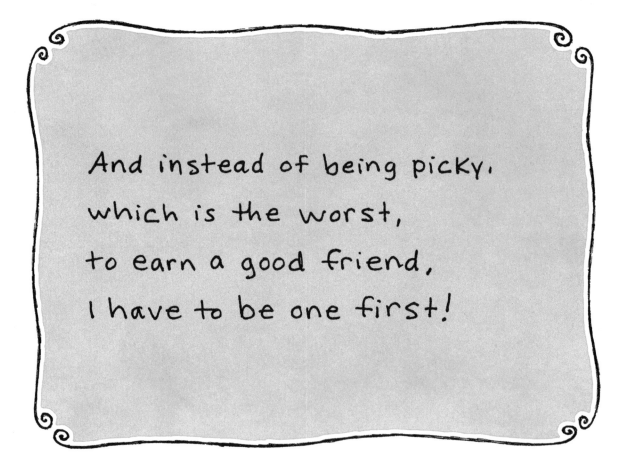

And instead of being picky,
which is the worst,
to earn a good friend,
I have to be one first!

windhillbooks

Other Books from Craig and Jeanna Kunce

Edrick the Inventor: Saturday is Cleaning Day

Edrick the Inventor: Spring is for Gardening

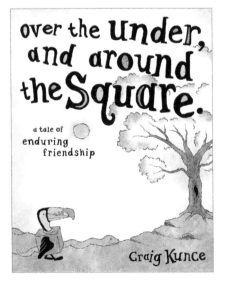

Over the Under, and around the Square

Trouble finds ME

Hope's Melody

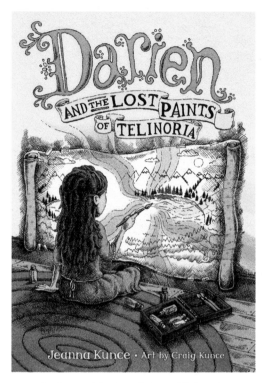

Darien and the Lost Paints of Telinoria

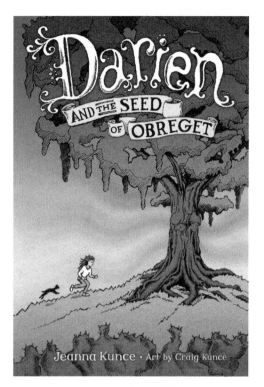

Darien and the Seed of Obreget

My Perfect Friend?

Very, Very, Afraid!

CPSIA information can be obtained
at www.ICGtesting.com
Printed in the USA
LVOW05s0124120916

504177LV00001B/1/P